JOSEPH·JOSLIN
MEMORIAL·LIBRARY

BORN   DIED
JAN. 23, 1776   JAN. 17, 1865
SETTLED IN WAITSFIELD
1798
THE GIFT OF HIS
GRANDSON
GEORGE·ALFRED JOSLIN
1913

Oh No, Noah!

· Johanna Hurwitz ·

OH NO, NOAH!

Illustrated by Mike Reed

SeaStar Books
New York

SEASTAR BOOKS
A division of NORTH-SOUTH BOOKS INC.

First published in the United States by SeaStar Books, a division of North-South Books Inc., New York.
Published simultaneously in Canada, Australia, and New Zealand by
North-South Books, an imprint of Nord-Süd Verlag AG, Gossau Zürich, Switzerland.

Library of Congress Cataloging-in-Publication Data is available.
The artwork for this book was prepared digitally.
Book design by Nicole Stanco de las Heras.

ISBN 1-58717-133-3 (reinforced trade edition)
1   3   5   7   9   RTE   10   8   6   4   2

Printed in U.S.A.

For more information about our books, and the authors and artists who create them,
visit our web site: www.northsouth.com

Oh yes, Juliet & Ethan!
This book's for you.

Contents

Oh No, Noah!

Chapter 1
An Unusual Gift

There was a loud and unexpected crash in the kitchen at 412 Rainbow Drive.

"Oh no," moaned Noah Baxter. He pushed his glasses up on his nose as he looked at the mess down by his feet.

Mrs. Baxter looked at the shattered glass on the kitchen floor. "Oh no, Noah," she sighed. "How did you do that?"

"It was an accident," said Noah. He was still standing exactly where he'd been when he'd dropped the box of drinking glasses.

"I was just moving the box from one place to another, and when I picked it up, it slipped and everything fell out. Maybe they didn't all break," Noah added, trying to be hopeful.

"Don't move," his mother instructed him. "You might step on some of the glass."

Noah remained in place while his mother carefully swept up all the shards of glass around him. "It's good Bunny is safely in her crib napping," Mrs. Baxter said. Bunny, whose real name was Bernice, was Noah's little sister. She was almost two years old.

Only a couple of days ago, on July 7, Noah's family had moved to this house. The furniture was in place now, but there were still dozens of boxes waiting to be unpacked.

That was why on such a hot day Noah was standing in the kitchen removing dishes from cartons.

"I'm getting tired," Noah complained. He wasn't sleepy tired, like Bunny, just tired of standing in one place and tired of helping his mother with the unpacking.

"Oh Noah, I'm tired, too," his mother agreed. "Let's take a break," she suggested as she threw the broken glass into the garbage. "I'll get us each a cold drink—if I can find something to drink from."

Noah sat down on a kitchen chair and looked at his fingers. They were dirty from the newspapers. Every dish the Baxters owned had been individually wrapped in newspaper so it wouldn't break. That was a waste of time, he thought. The glasses had broken anyhow, and now everything had to be unwrapped and put into the kitchen cupboards. For a moment Noah considered washing his hands, but he knew his hands would only get dirty all over again. It didn't seem worth the effort.

Besides this large kitchen, the new house was big enough so that now Noah had his own bedroom and didn't have to share with Bunny anymore. This house had an upstairs as well as a downstairs, a working fireplace, and a small backyard. There was also a basement, where the furnace was located. It was all so amazing to someone who had spent his entire life in a cramped city apartment. It was only the thought of entering a new school filled with all new faces in September that made Noah feel a little anxious.

"Here," said Mrs. Baxter, handing her son a glass of lemonade with ice cubes. "This will cool you off."

The glass was cold. Noah rubbed it against his forehead. Even without opening his mouth, it was making him feel better. In a few gulps, he drained the lemonade from the glass.

"Good," Noah said, smiling at his mother. He took an ice cube in his mouth and crunched down on it.

"Oh no, Noah, please," Mrs. Baxter said. "You know I can't stand that sound. My teeth ache just from hearing you chew on ice cubes. And it's bad for your teeth as well."

"Sorry," Noah said. He never could understand why such a simple thing upset his mother. But he usually tried to remember not to do it when she was in the room.

The doorbell rang and Mrs. Baxter went to see who was there. It gave Noah a chance to quickly chew one more of the ice cubes.

"Look," his mother said, returning to the kitchen. "That was the postal truck. It's another housewarming gift for us."

"Maybe that's why it's so hot," said Noah. Many of their friends and relatives were sending housewarming presents. The last few days had almost seemed like they were having a birthday or Christmas in the summer. Unfortunately, the gifts that they were getting were pretty boring—a set of wineglasses, a ceramic teapot, a crystal vase. These breakable gifts came with more packing than present inside the box.

Noah watched with anticipation while his mother opened the package. Maybe one of these days someone would give them a present that he could enjoy, too. But this package contained a ceramic pitcher. Boring. Except to Bunny, who liked throwing the Styrofoam packing into the air.

A second gift arrived that evening. When Noah's father returned home from work, he took a huge carton out of the car.

"What's that?" asked Noah eagerly, holding the door open for his father. Such a big box should surely hold something worthwhile.

"I have absolutely no idea," his father said. Noah thought he must be joking.

"Well, let's see what's inside," his mother said. She had been busy cutting up vegetables for salad. She stopped to examine the box.

Bunny pulled herself up off the floor so she could see what was in the package, too.

"For me?" she asked hopefully.

"This is a gift for our whole family from Mr. Powers," Mr. Baxter announced, as he pulled off sticky brown tape that was holding the box firmly shut.

"Wasn't that nice of him to give us a present," said Noah's mom. Mr. Powers was her husband's supervisor at work.

Next, Noah's dad pulled out crumpled-up newspapers that were inside the box.

"It must be more dishes," said Noah with disappointment.

Mr. Baxter removed the last of the newspaper from the carton. Inside was something brown and hairy and . . .

"Oh my heavens!" shrieked Noah's mom, looking over her husband's shoulder.

"What is it?" asked Noah, pushing closer

to get a better look. Something in his mother's tone made him suspect this was not another package of wineglasses.

Mr. Baxter removed a large animal head, complete with antlers and glass eyes from the box. It had once been attached to a deer. Noah had seen live ones at the zoo back in the city. But those all had bodies attached to them.

Bunny gave a howl of terror and toddled as fast as she could out of the room.

"I don't know whether to laugh or scream myself," called Mrs. Baxter, as she ran off to comfort her daughter.

Noah looked at the head. "I'd rather have a whole animal," he told his father. The head didn't scare him, but the idea of cutting it off from the rest of its body seemed gross.

"Stuffed like this?" asked Mr. Baxter.

"No. Alive. Who wants a dead head for a present?" he said.

"Well, some people hang these heads on the wall," Noah's dad explained.

"Why?"

"They think it's a good decoration. If they shot the deer themselves, they can show off what they did."

"I'd never shoot a deer," said Noah.

"I wouldn't either," said his dad. "But what in the world are we going to do with this thing?"

"Please don't hang it up," Noah begged him. He hated the thought of spoiling their new home with the glass eyes of the dead deer head appearing to stare at them all the time.

"Don't worry. I have no intention of putting it up on any of our walls. I wonder why in the world George Powers gave this to me. It's a very weird gift!"

"We could hide it away in the basement," suggested Noah.

"Great idea," said his father. "Isn't it lucky that we moved to a house with a big basement for storing things?"

Noah accompanied his father down into the basement. It occurred to him that if they hadn't moved to the new house, they would never have received the head, and then they wouldn't need the basement for storing it.

"I'll just put the box here," said Mr. Baxter, shoving it into a corner. Noah backed up and bumped into a pile of boxes nearby. The top box tumbled down, spilling out its contents.

"Oh no, Noah," said his dad, as the two

of them looked down on the hundreds of photographs on the basement floor. It was Noah's mom's plan to someday put them into albums. Now Noah looked at his whole life spread before him on the floor of the basement. Well, at least nothing had broken, he thought.

Chapter 2

A Head in the Hedge

Noah's new home had a front and a back door. The front one faced Rainbow Drive. The back door opened onto a small grassy yard. To Noah, this space was almost like having a tiny park behind his house. There weren't any swings or climbing bars or benches. Still, the thought that the hedges surrounding the property, the two tall trees, and each blade of grass and pebble belonged to his family was hard to believe. Why, even the ants that he watched climbing out of a tiny anthill belonged to them.

Sometimes Noah played with Bunny out in the yard. He rolled a ball toward her and she learned to roll it back. Other times, he blew bubbles for her to chase. But often, Noah was out in the yard by himself. He would sit on the back steps and read or use his toy microscope to study bits of plants or bugs that he found in the yard. He wished that he had a friend to be there with him. He had several friends back at his old home and someday they were all going to come to visit.

"You need some friends around here," his mother told him.

"I guess I'll get them when school starts," Noah said. He hoped he was right. One never knew about friends.

On the first day of the second week that Noah lived on Rainbow Drive, he was out in the backyard. He felt a tickle in his left nostril and rubbed inside his nose with his finger.

"Yuck!" a voice called out.

Noah looked around, and through the hedge that separated his yard from the one behind his house, he saw the head of a girl.

"Who are you?" he demanded of the head.

The head, and the body it was attached to, pulled some branches apart and crawled into Noah's yard. She stood up. "Were you picking your nose?" the girl asked.

"Were you spying on me?" Noah demanded to know.

The girl was just about the same height as Noah and she looked about his age. She grinned at him.

"I never pick my nose," Noah told her. "And even if I did, so what? This is my property."

"That means you probably were. You're Noah, right?" the girl asked him.

"No, I wasn't," said Noah. "And how do you know who I am?" he asked.

"I heard your mother calling to you," the girl explained. "I live back there," she added, pointing to the house behind the hedge.

"Have you been watching since we moved in?" asked Noah. He tried to remember all the times in the past week that he had been in the yard and what he had done there. This girl could have watched him scratch other body parts or who knows what.

"I just got home last night," the girl said. "My family was on a trip to Chicago. That's where my grandparents live," she explained.

Noah gave a sigh of relief. This girl had never seen him before.

"Were you ever there?" she asked him.

"Where?"

"In Chicago, silly. Were you ever there?" the girl asked again.

"No."

"I've been there hundreds of times," she boasted.

"So who are you anyway?" Noah asked. "What's your name?"

"Maureen Olivia Alice Patricia Yeats," the girl said. It seemed like an awful lot of names for one person. "You can call me Mo," she added. "Most people do."

"Okay," said Noah. "It would take all week to say the rest."

Mo grinned again. "Everyone in my family has long names. My big sister is Erin

Eileen Elizabeth Anne Yeats and my little sister is Kathleen Theresa Mary Josephine Yeats."

"Don't you have any brothers?" Noah asked hopefully.

"Nope."

"Well, how old are you anyway?" Noah wanted to know.

"Eight. Almost. My birthday is at the beginning of September. Just before school starts."

"I'm eight already," said Noah. At least he had one advantage over this girl.

"Can I see your rabbit?" Mo asked Noah.

"I don't have a rabbit. I don't have any pets. Do you?"

"You must have a rabbit. I heard your mother talking about it this morning," Mo insisted.

Noah looked at his neighbor. She seemed to think she knew everything, but this time she was really wrong. "There are no rabbits here," he told her again. But suddenly he started smiling. "What did you hear my mother say?" he asked.

"She said *I'm going to keep bunny inside this morning.*"

"Bunny is my sister," said Noah.

"You have a rabbit for a sister?" asked Mo.

"Of course not. She's a little girl named Bernice and we call her *Bunny* just like people call you Mo instead of all your other names."

"I wish you had a rabbit," said Mo with disappointment. Then she smiled. "I wish I had a cat," she added. "Instead, I have a *Kitty* at my house. That's what we call my little sister."

"It sounds like a zoo around here. But all we have are these ants," said Noah, pointing to the anthill he'd been studying.

"Can I see inside your house?" Mo asked. "I've been inside hundreds of times when the Lewises lived here. But I want to see what it looks like now."

The Lewis family were the people who formerly owned the Baxter home. Noah wasn't sure he wanted this nosy girl looking around inside his house, but couldn't think of a good reason to keep her out. "All right," he agreed.

They went inside together. Within forty-five minutes, Mo had learned lots about Noah, and he had learned lots about her, too. Mo's older sister was off at Girl Scout camp. Her little sister was just a few months older than Bunny. Best of all, Mo had a bunch of friends that she promised Noah he could meet. A couple of them would be going into third grade with them in the fall. And they were boys!

Mrs. Baxter offered Noah and his guest some juice and cookies. Then Noah gave Mo a full tour of his new home. He showed off his new room. "I share my bedroom with Erin," Mo told him. She wasn't complaining, just stating a fact. "We sleep on bunk beds. I have to sleep on the bottom," she said. That was a complaint.

They walked through each room upstairs and down, even the basement. When they got down there, Noah thought of something else to show Mo.

"You want to see something weird?" he asked her.

"Yeah. What?" asked Mo.

"I'll show you. But don't scream when you see it."

"What do you have? Do you keep snakes in your basement?" asked Mo.

"I told you I don't have any pets," Noah reminded her, as he led the way toward the pile of cartons in one corner of the basement. "Close your eyes," he said, feeling pleased that he could show her something unusual.

"Why?"

"Because I said so," Noah told her.

"Is this a trick?" asked Mo suspiciously.

"No. Just close your eyes," said Noah again.

Mo closed her eyes and Noah opened the carton that his father had stored in the basement. He lifted out the contents and held it up. "Okay. You can look now."

Mo opened her eyes and let out a shout of delight. "Wow! Lucky you! Where did you buy that? Is it real or is it plastic?"

"It was a real deer and now it's a real dead deer," Noah explained. "We didn't buy it. It's a gift. But it's a weird gift and that's why we keep it down here."

"Let me touch it," said Mo, coming toward the deer head. She stroked the hair and rubbed the antlers. "Neat," she said, sounding very envious.

"Neat? Strange is more like it," Noah said. "No one in my family likes it. That's why it's hidden down here. It's not exactly a useful gift." But even as he said that to Mo, he realized that the deer head had been useful after all. It was the first and only thing he'd had to show off that had really impressed his neighbor.

Chapter 3
Tricks

Before she went home for lunch, Mo promised Noah that she would arrange for him to meet the other kids their age who lived nearby. Sure enough, a couple of hours later, there was a knock on the back door. Mrs. Baxter opened it and there stood Mo.

"Everybody's waiting for Noah," she said.

"Everybody?" asked Mrs. Baxter with surprise.

"Everybody?" Noah echoed. It would have been much more to his liking to meet new kids one at a time. This sounded like walking into a full classroom at school.

It turned out that it wasn't quite that bad. Counting Mo and himself, there were five kids in all—Peter and Andy, who would both be going into third grade with Mo and Noah, and a girl named Jessica. She was bigger than all of them, but it turned out she was the youngest. She was also Peter's sister.

"I forgot to ask you what kind of tricks you can do," Mo said to Noah, as they all sat in her backyard, which was just like his.

"Tricks? I don't know any tricks," said Noah.

"You must know some trick," said Jessica.

"We all know at least one," Peter added.

Noah squirmed. He looked through a

space in the hedge and saw his own house across the way. In fact, he could see Bunny's pink sunsuit as she ran around inside their yard. He could hear his mother talking to her. But even though his family was so near, Noah felt alone. He, of all these kids, didn't know any tricks. This was a sort of test from them. He stalled for time because he knew he was bound to fail.

"What kind of tricks do you do?" he asked Andy.

"Listen to this," Andy replied. He stuck his two hands together, and holding them to his mouth, he let out a piercing whistle.

"Wow. That's louder than ever," said Jessica admiringly.

"Teach us again," Mo begged.

Andy held his two hands close out. "Now hold them together so that there's only one small hole to blow into."

Mo, Jessica, Peter, and Noah followed the directions.

"Okay, now blow," said Andy.

There was the sound of air blowing from four mouths, but no whistle.

"Look, I'll show you one more time," said Andy. He repeated his instructions. "You have to tilt your mouth so the air goes up," he remembered to add this time.

The four students all blew together. Again, there was the sound of air coming from their mouths, but no whistle.

"You can't let the air escape through your fingers," Andy warned. "It won't work that way."

"I never can get it," Mo complained. "I've tried over and over again, but nothing happens when I blow."

"You'll just have to practice more," said Andy. "It's easy when you know how. My father taught me, and it took forever until I could do it. But it's like riding a bike. Before we could do it, it seemed impossible. But now it's so easy for all of us."

"I do have a trick," Noah suddenly shouted with great relief. "I can ride my bike with only one hand."

"That's not much," said Peter. "I can ride my bike with no hands. And that's not even my trick."

"Oh," said Noah with disappointment. He suddenly wondered why he'd never even tried riding with only one hand. "So what is your trick?" he asked Peter.

"Look," said Peter. He crossed his eyes.

"Aren't you afraid they'll get stuck like that?" Noah asked.

"Naw," said Peter. "I can burp at will, too." He gave a demonstration.

Everyone laughed except Noah. This

was getting serious, he thought. He'd better come up with something.

"So can't you do anything?" Mo asked Noah.

"Sure I can," said Noah, stalling for time. "But I want to see what you can do first."

"Okay, wait a minute," she said, and she ran into the house.

Noah hoped she'd take her time. He still had to figure out something that he could do that the others couldn't.

Mo returned holding three plums. Maybe she would put them all in her mouth at once, Noah thought.

"Watch this," Mo said. Instead of putting the plums in her mouth, she threw them up in the air and began juggling them.

Peter let out a whistle of appreciation.

"I can even do this with eggs," Mo said proudly. "But my mother gets worried. And

she hardly ever lets me do it. She says she doesn't like to waste good food, and if I dropped an egg, that would be the end of it." Mo shrugged. "When I grow up and no one can tell me what to do, I'll juggle all the eggs I want. Right now I'm working on juggling four things at once. Probably in another week or two, I'll be able to do it," she bragged.

"Who taught you this?" asked Noah.

"My uncle. He can juggle half a dozen things at once. He's super."

Noah thought about his family. His father didn't have a special way of whistling. His uncles couldn't juggle. No wonder he didn't have any tricks to show off.

"What do you do?" Noah asked Jessica.

"I can do something better than stand on my head," Jessica told him.

"What?" asked Noah.

Jessica whispered to Mo. "I'll be right back," Mo said, running into the house again.

"Bring back those plums," Peter called to her. "We could eat them."

But Mo and the plums were gone. Noah racked his brain. He couldn't think of any tricks at all. He vaguely recalled that years ago his grandfather had shown him a card trick. But then he didn't do it for a long time and he forgot it. How could he keep up with these new friends if he didn't have a special trick to show off like they did?

Mo came out of the house holding a book.

"What's that for?" asked Noah.

"Just watch," said Jessica. She picked a

spot on the grass and proceeded to stand on her head. Then Mo brought the book over and laid it on the ground next to Jessica.

"*Whoever has made a voyage up the Hudson River must remember the Catskill Mountains, rising mag . . . mag . . . mag . . .* See, I can read standing on my head," said Jessica proudly.

"Except when there's a hard word," Mo pointed out.

"That was a word I wouldn't be able to read right side up either," Jessica admitted, as she put her feet back on the ground again and sat up.

Noah reached for the book and looked at it. It was called *Rip Van Winkle*. He'd never heard of that book before. He looked at the word that Jessica had gotten stuck on.

"Mag-ni-fi-cent-ly," he sounded out.

"Hey. I can read big words. Does that count as a trick?"

"Of course not," said Peter. "This isn't school. Our tricks are all fun things. Not school things."

Noah was in a sweat. He was about to admit that he didn't have a trick after all. Maybe they would give him time to learn one. It wasn't his fault that he didn't have one. Where he used to live, the kids never did tricks.

Mo's mother came outside carrying a tray of glasses and a pitcher of fruit punch. "I think you can all use a cold drink on a day like this," she told them.

Noah gratefully took the glass of punch. He listened to the ice cubes clinking around inside his glass.

Peter swallowed some of his punch.

"Okay," he said to Noah, "so what else can you do? Besides riding your bike with one hand and reading hard words. You must know something."

"Maybe we could teach him to do all of our tricks," offered Mo.

Noah smiled at her for coming to his rescue. He wouldn't mind being the student of all these kids. It would be neat to juggle and stand on his head and make a loud whistle. He crunched down on the ice cube in his mouth.

"Can you do this?" he asked suddenly.

"Do what?" asked Jessica.

"Chew ice cubes?"

"I never tried," said Peter. "Besides, that's pretty dumb."

"Yeah," said Andy. "Who'd want to do that?"

"Chewing ice cubes is silly," Mo agreed.

They all nodded their heads in agreement.

Noah flushed with annoyance and embarrassment. Maybe chewing ice cubes wasn't such a great trick, he thought. After all, his mother didn't even want him to do it. But what made crossing one's eyes or burping at will better tricks? What was the point of reading while standing on one's head? he wondered. What was the big deal about throwing plums up in the air? All their tricks were dumb, too. He looked around at the other kids. He guessed they wouldn't want to be his friends now.

"Wait a minute," said Mo. "Noah has something better than a trick that he can show you."

"What?" asked Peter.

What? Noah wondered himself.

"We have to go down to his basement to

see it. Come on, everyone." And suddenly, to Noah's amazement, Mo was shoving everyone through the hedge.

"Hi there," said a startled Mrs. Baxter to the group of children who suddenly appeared in the yard. "Are you having a good time together?"

"Yep," Mo replied. She opened the back door and marched inside Noah's house. Everyone followed her, including Noah. By now he'd caught on to what Mo wanted him to show off. He turned on the switch for the basement light. They all went down the stairs.

"What's so special down here?" Jessica asked.

"You have to close your eyes first," Mo told the other kids. She was acting just the way Noah had when he introduced her to the deer head earlier. "Then you'll see."

Noah walked over to the carton and took out the head.

"Okay. You can look now," Mo said.

"Wow!"

Peter crossed his eyes to show his surprise. "Can we touch it?" asked Jessica, moving toward the head.

"This is better than a trick any day," said Peter, stroking the antlers.

Noah stood tall and proud as he held the deer head. Finally, he had something that he could show off, too.

"What's this doing down in your basement anyhow?" asked Andy.

"It was a housewarming gift, but we don't really like it. It scares my sister," Noah explained.

"I know what we should do," said Mo.

"What?" asked Jessica.

"We should give this poor head a funeral."

"Oh yes," Jessica agreed at once. All of the kids liked the idea. Even Noah. He wasn't certain that his parents would approve of burying their housewarming present, but he couldn't resist being the owner of this center attraction. Without his deer head, there could be no funeral.

Chapter 4
The Funeral

Noah had many hours to think about the funeral, because Mo decided they should wait and hold it the following morning.

"Where are we going to bury it?" he asked her. He certainly didn't want to put the deer head in the ground of his new backyard.

"We'll take it over to Andy's house," Mo announced. "He's got the biggest yard of all of us."

"Cool," said Andy, beaming. He was pleased about that plan.

Noah almost discussed the upcoming funeral with his parents. He wasn't one hundred percent certain that it was the right thing to do. But since the whole family had agreed they didn't want the deer head, he figured they couldn't object to getting rid of it. In fact, he told himself, burying the head of the poor dead deer seemed like a really decent thing to do.

At suppertime, Mr. Baxter commented, "I hear you've made a lot of new friends today."

"Yeah," Noah said through a mouth full of corn on the cob.

"Will you be seeing them tomorrow?" Noah's mother asked him.

That was the moment when Noah

could have explained about the funeral. But it was also the moment when Bunny overturned her plate of food—the three older Baxters all bent down and picked up the cut-up pieces of meat loaf and carrots and corn from the floor. Noah made up his mind. He wouldn't say anything about the funeral ceremony. It would just be something between him and his new friends.

*   *   *

Mo came through the backyard at ten o'clock the next morning. She sat down at the kitchen table and made herself at home talking to Noah's mother and Bunny. While they were occupied, Noah went down to the basement and brought up the carton. He quietly opened the front door and left the box and its contents on the doorstep. Then he went back to get Mo.

"See you around," she called to Noah's mother and sister.

"Where are you going to be?" Mrs. Baxter asked.

"We're going over to Andy's house. He lives just around the corner on West Wind Street," Mo explained.

"Okay," said Mrs. Baxter, "have fun."

Noah and Mo went out the front door and Noah picked up the carton.

"I don't think you're supposed to have fun at funerals," Noah said to Mo. He was relieved that he'd managed to get the deer head out of his house so easily. But he felt uncomfortable about it, too. It was the first time he'd ever done something that sneaky. He didn't count chewing ice cubes when his mother wasn't in the room. This seemed much more serious.

"It's not like we knew this deer personally," said Mo. "We can't feel the same sort of sadness that we would if he had been a pet that we loved."

"Right," Noah agreed, thinking it over.

Andy's house was very near and his backyard seemed very big compared to Noah's and Mo's.

Peter and Jessica were waiting for them together with Andy. Andy was the only one who seemed dressed for a funeral. He was wearing a black T-shirt, although it said *There's no burger like Joe's burgers* on the back and had a picture of a giant hamburger on the front. Noah had only been to one funeral in his life. It was for his grandfather, and he remembered that most of the people who attended wore black clothes.

"I want to see the deer again," said Jessica, coming up to Noah.

"Poor deer," said Peter.

"Poor dear," said Jessica, stroking the deer's face. "She looks so sad."

"She's a he," Noah pointed out. "*He*s have antlers, not *she*s. And he doesn't look sad. He looks dead."

"Well, of course. He *is* dead," said Peter, daringly sticking a finger into one of the glass eyes.

"Show some respect," said Mo, pushing Peter away. Noah closed the box.

Andy had gotten two shovels ready for digging a hole.

"I'll dig first," Mo announced. "And Noah can help me."

"Why you?" asked Andy. "It's my yard."

"It was my idea to have a funeral. And I was the one who discovered that Noah had the head," said Mo, holding on to one of the shovels.

Noah stood watching them argue. It would take a lot of digging to make the hole big enough. He knew they'd all have a turn.

"Let's choose," he suggested.

"Yeah," Jessica backed him up.

So they did a few rounds of *once, twice, three shoot*, and eventually Peter and Andy began the digging. Mo had her turn. Noah got his. It wasn't easy making such a big hole. And in the end, Jessica turned out to be the best digger in the group.

"You could do this for a living when you grow up," suggested Mo.

"There are other things to dig holes for besides coffins," Andy pointed out.

"Like digging for gold," offered Peter.

"Or clams."

"Buried treasure."

"Worms for fishing."

Unfortunately, although they spotted a couple of worms, Jessica did not find any gold, clams, or buried treasure.

"We forgot to get a marker so nobody will dig up this space after the funeral," said Mo thoughtfully. She looked around and spotted a small pile of bricks near the house. They were left over from when Andy's father had built an outdoor barbecue.

"This will do," she said, grabbing one of the bricks.

Finally they were ready for the funeral to begin. Everyone rubbed their dirty, sweaty hands on their clothes.

"Who's in charge?" asked Andy.

"It was my idea," said Mo.

"It's my deer head," Noah reminded everyone.

"I dug the biggest amount of the hole," said Jessica.

"We'll take turns then," said Noah. He felt like the peacekeeper of the group.

He started things off by reciting the only prayer he knew: "Now I lay me down to sleep, I pray the Lord my soul to keep. If I should die before I wake, I pray the Lord my soul to take."

"Deers don't have souls," whispered Jessica.

"How do you know?" Noah whispered back.

"Besides, he probably wasn't even sleeping when he was killed," said Jessica a little louder. "I don't think that's a very good prayer."

"Well, you take a turn. What do you want to say?" asked Noah in somewhat of a huff.

Jessica didn't know.

"We could sing 'God Bless America.' That's what they sang when my grandfather died," Noah suddenly remembered. "He was in the army and they put an American flag over his coffin."

"We don't even have a coffin," said Peter.

"I know. I know what to sing," shouted Jessica. She stood tall and began "Doe a deer, a female deer . . . "

The others joined in. It did seem to be exactly the right song to sing at this time, even if the deer was a male and not a doe at all.

Then Noah suddenly remembered

another appropriate song. "Oh, give me a home where the buffalo roam, and the deer and the antelope play. . . . " There were more words, but he could only remember a few of them. He hummed the rest of the song and the others joined in.

When the humming stopped, Mo reached for the head and pulled it out of the carton. Then she put it into the hole. All the children were silent. It was the most serious moment of the funeral.

Noah looked at the deer head lying in the hole. He wondered if they should have used the carton as a coffin. But it was a big carton and it would take a lot more digging to make the hole large enough to include it. What difference did it make? he wondered. The deer wouldn't care if its head got dirty now.

Everyone had a turn shoveling soil over

the deer head until it was covered. One part of the antler poked through the soil. Andy walked over and stomped on it with his foot. Nothing happened at first, but he did it again and the antler snapped off. Noah shuddered at the sound.

The last shovels full of dirt covered up the antler. Then they all stamped on the ground and threw bits of grass and dandelions on top. Noah took the brick and put it on the center of the grave. The funeral was over.

Noah still wasn't sure what his parents would say if they heard about the funeral. Chances were they never would. He wasn't going to talk about it and he didn't think they were in any hurry to go looking for that old head.

"Well, my little sister's not going to be

scared of that deer head ever again," he announced to the others.

"Yes. But now that the head is underground, will it frighten the worms?" Jessica wanted to know.

Chapter 5
Noah's Mark

So now Noah had a bunch of new friends. A couple of days later he went out skating with Mo, Andy, Peter, and Jessica. They set off to skate the four-block square that surrounded his house. There was his street, Rainbow Drive, and around the corner was Andy's street, West Wind. If they kept going they would reach Sunrise Road, where Mo's house was, and finally, Shadow

Street, where Peter and Jessica lived. The names of the streets sounded a bit like they were living in the middle of a weather forecast!

Noah's mother liked the idea that the children could visit with one another, or today skate around and around, without crossing any streets. It was ideal. Except today there was a problem.

When they got to the corner of Sunrise and Shadow, the ground had been dug up. A cement mixer was there, and two men were getting ready to put down fresh new cement on the walk in front of 209 Shadow Street.

The kids watched for a couple of minutes.

"That looks like fun," Noah said to one of the men who was smoothing the cement.

"Yeah," Andy agreed.

"Do you need any help?" Noah asked the men hopefully.

"Nope. And you kids better not mark up this cement when we're finished," one of the men replied.

"Come on," said Mo. "We don't need to skate in a circle. We can just turn around and go back the way we came."

The four others followed her lead and about-faced, skating to the corner of West Wind Street, where Mo stopped. "That man was mean," she said. "Why did he have to say that about messing up his cement? We hadn't even thought of doing it. But now I think we should."

"Yeah," Peter agreed.

"What would we do?" asked Jessica.

Mo shrugged. "We could each write our name," she suggested.

"That would be neat," said Andy.

"There are too many of us," said Noah. "I don't think we should all do it."

"We don't all have to do it," said Mo. "It was you he told to keep away."

"Naw. I don't really want to," said Noah.

"It was like he was daring you. You've got to do it," said Andy.

"Yeah, Andy's right. Write your name in the cement!" said Peter.

"Well, that's easy for you to say. Because Peter is a more popular name than Noah. There are probably lots of Peters living around here. I bet I'm the only Noah for blocks. I'm not putting my name into the wet cement. I could get into big trouble."

"Then don't put your name. Write your initials or the year," said Mo.

"That's a good idea," said Jessica.

Noah didn't think it was a good idea at all.

"Are you scared to do it?" asked Peter.

"No," lied Noah.

"Let's keep skating," said Mo. "Then we can see when those workmen finish up."

Noah hoped the men would stay a long time. If the cement dried quickly, he wouldn't be able to write anything. It was dumb of him to have asked if they needed help. He knew they didn't, but he'd said it anyhow.

They all skated until they came upon the new cement from the opposite direction. The men were gathering their tools. It looked like they were getting ready to leave.

"About-face," Mo commanded her friends.

"This sounds like we're in the army," complained Noah.

Jessica giggled and gave a salute. No one else saluted, but everyone turned around.

It took another few minutes for them to approach the sidewalk from the opposite direction. This time the men were gone. But there were strips of yellow plastic tape marking off the area.

"Okay," said Mo. "Now you can do it."

Noah looked down at his hands. "How can I do it? With my fingers?"

Peter picked up a wooden ice-cream pop stick that was in the gutter. "You can use this."

Noah took the stick. "Listen," he said, "this is a dumb idea."

"No. That guy insulted you," said Mo. "You have to do it."

"I don't feel insulted," said Noah. "I feel . . . "

"Scared?" asked Peter.

"No," said Noah. "I feel silly. I know what year it is. Why do I have to write it into the cement?"

"To prove that the guy didn't scare you off. And besides, there's always writing in fresh cement. People do it all the time," Mo pointed out.

"Well, why me? If you think it should be here, one of you do it," Noah said, looking at the other kids.

"I'll do it if you're scared," offered Mo.

Noah looked around. There was no one about on the street. He didn't see anyone looking out of the windows of the house. "Okay," he said. "Here goes."

He bent down and carefully began inscribing the year while his friends stood watching him. The cement was already beginning to harden and he had to press heavily with the wooden stick. **2, 0. . .**

"Look out!" shouted Peter.

Noah looked up. He saw that the front door of the house had opened and a man was hurrying toward him. "Hey, stop that!" the man shouted at him. Noah heard the sound of skates on the sidewalk as Mo, Jessica, Peter, and Andy made their getaway. But Noah felt paralyzed. The man had seen him.

"What do you think you're doing?" the man yelled at him.

"I was just going to write the year," Noah admitted.

"On my sidewalk? Do you know how much I paid to have this walk freshly paved?" the man demanded.

"No," said Noah. How would a kid know a thing like that? "Maybe I could smooth it over," he offered.

"I don't think your smoothing would be good enough. This part of the walk is spoiled. It will never look freshly paved like the rest," the man grumbled.

"I'm sorry," said Noah. He wondered if he should offer to pay to have the cement workers return. But he didn't know where he'd get the money, so he kept his mouth closed. Instead, he stood looking guiltily down at his handiwork.

"I can't believe you did it. The men were here only five minutes ago." The man bent down and looked at the numbers that were carved into his walk. "So, was it fun?" he asked.

That was a weird question, Noah thought. "It seemed like it would be fun. But I think I was afraid I'd get caught, so that spoiled it," he admitted.

"And you did get caught," the man said. "Give me that stick." Noah handed it over. "I always wanted to do it myself when I was your age. And it's never too late."

Then, to Noah's amazement the man bent down, and next to the existing **20** he made a **9**.

"There," he said. "The year will change before you know it. But my address won't."

Noah and the man admired the numbers: **209**.

"Does this mean you aren't angry at me?" Noah asked.

"It means I was a kid once myself," the man said. "Go home. And when you see your friends, tell them that they were all cowards not to stay around and face the music with you."

Noah nodded his head. "I guess everyone's a coward sometime," he said, remembering how he'd felt earlier. He looked down at the numbers. For the rest of his life he could look at that 2 and the 0 and remember that he'd made them. He'd made his mark in this new cement.

"So long," he called. Then he skated off to look for Mo, Jessica, Andy, and Peter.

"Did you get in big trouble?" asked Mo when she saw him.

Noah shrugged his shoulders.

"Did you tell on us?" Peter asked him.

"What do you think?" Noah replied.

"You told the guy our names?" asked Andy, looking nervous.

"Is that what you would have done?" Noah asked him.

Andy was quiet for a second. "I don't know," he admitted.

"Well, I didn't tell on you," Noah said.

"Gee. Thanks," said Peter, looking relieved.

"You're a pal," said Mo, slapping Noah on the back.

"Well, just because I didn't tell this time doesn't mean I won't some other time. You can't just do bad things and run off," Noah told his friends.

"Or skate off either," said Jessica.

"You're right," Mo said. "We let you down. I'm sorry. You're sorry, too, aren't you?" she asked the others.

They all agreed.

"Okay. We won't do anything like that again," Mo promised Noah.

Then they all skated off like nothing had happened. But Noah realized that this incident, even more than the funeral, had really cemented his friendship with Mo, Jessica, Andy, and Peter.

And the next day, when he happened to walk past 209 Shadow Street, Noah noticed that a stray cat had left a series of paw prints on the freshly made sidewalk. Obviously, he wasn't the only one leaving his mark around here.

Chapter 6
The Wading Pool

On Saturday morning, Noah went on a shopping trip with his dad. There were so many things they needed these days— picture hooks, a hose, a trash can, door stoppers, hedge clippers, a barbecue grill, and a huge bag of charcoal. Noah was looking forward to outdoor barbecues.

There was a midsummer sale on plastic wading pools. "This would be perfect for

Bunny to play in," said Noah's dad, as he put one in their cart. The pool was made of bright red plastic and had to be inflated using a bicycle pump. "You could splash around in it, too," he suggested to his son.

"Nah. That's for babies," said Noah. He wouldn't want Mo and the other kids seeing him do that. You'd never find a kid his size playing in a baby wading pool. Maybe his father would drive him and his friends to the community swimming pool in the afternoon, he thought hopefully. Mo had told him all about it.

Back home on Rainbow Drive, Mr. Baxter set to work at once inflating the wading pool. It took a lot of pumping, and after a bit, he gave Noah a chance to work on it, too. It was fun at first, but before long Noah was in a sweat and the pool wasn't much bigger. Noah removed his T-shirt, which was sticking to his back, and pushed his glasses back up on his nose. Now that he was just wearing a pair of shorts, he felt much more comfortable.

"What are you doing?" a voice demanded to know.

It was Mo, once again peeking through the hedge that separated their two yards. "Pumping up this baby pool. It's for my sister," Noah added quickly, wanting to be sure she knew it wasn't something he'd be caught dead in. "Want to help us?" he asked.

"Sure," said Mo, and in a moment, she had the pump in her hand. Slowly, with three pairs of hands and a lot of effort on everyone's part, the pool reached its full size. Noah looked with surprise at the pool.

All blown up, it was bigger than he had expected.

Mr. Baxter attached the new hose to an outside tap and turned on the water to fill the pool. "If I fill it now, the water can warm up in the sun and be a comfortable temperature when Bunny wakes from her nap," he said.

Noah stuck his hand in the water. It felt cool on his hot sweaty hand. He put his other hand in the water, too, and then rubbed his flushed face with his wet hands. That felt good, too. And since his feet felt hot inside his sneakers, he sat down on the ground and took off his shoes and socks as well.

Mo did the same thing. "Boy, my feet were boiling hot!" she complained, as she and Noah stuck their feet inside the pool.

It felt really great. Mo kicked her right foot up and down, splashing around the water. Noah kicked both of his feet, causing a splash twice as big.

"Are you playing in that wading pool?" a voice called out. It was Jessica. Behind her were Peter and Andy.

"Of course not," said Noah, turning around and shaking water off of himself. Even with Mo in the pool beside him, he worried about losing the status he had gained with these new friends. "We're just fooling around. Only babies play in wading pools," he reminded them.

"Well, can we fool around in there, too?" asked Andy.

"Sure," said Noah.

Jessica removed her sandals and jumped into the little wading pool. In a second,

Peter and Andy had their shoes off and were jumping into the pool, too. Soon, all five of them were sopping wet and there was hardly any water left inside the pool. So Noah went and turned on the hose again and refilled it.

The five of them lay down in the sun to dry off a bit.

"Babies are lucky," said Andy. "They get to play in wading pools. They don't need to hang around waiting for someone to drive them to a real swimming pool."

"Yeah," agreed Jessica. "We're so big, we can't pretend to swim in little wading pools anymore the way a baby can."

Mo grunted in agreement. "Wading is for babies," she said, getting up. She stepped back into the wading pool and walked across. "Look at me! I'm like

Moses crossing through the Red Sea," she proclaimed.

"The water is supposed to part in the middle," Jessica pointed out.

"That's not a sea and it's not red," said Peter.

"I'm going home," Mo called, jumping out of the wading pool. She rushed through the hedge and ran toward her house.

"Why'd she go?" Noah asked the others. He wondered if Peter had made her angry.

But Mo was back quickly. "Don't look. Close your eyes," she instructed everyone, and the kids all shut their eyes. Noah expected to be splashed with water. Why else would Mo tell them not to peek?

There was no splash. "Okay. Now you can open them," she called out. "Look!" She pointed to the wading pool.

At first no one knew what Mo was

pointing to. But a closer inspection showed that the redness of the water wasn't just a reflection from the red plastic. "How did you do that?" Peter wanted to know when he realized that the water was no longer colorless.

"I made the Red Sea," said Mo, holding up a small bottle. "I used my mother's food coloring. She has a whole set of colors that she uses when she makes frosting for our birthday cakes. She made a huge cake with green frosting for St. Patrick's Day, but she's never even used this red bottle. Now I'm really going to be like Moses crossing the Red Sea," she said proudly, as she climbed back into the pool and walked across. Mo walked back and forth through the water in the pool while her friends watched and cheered.

Suddenly, Noah noticed something.

"Hey," he shouted. "Look at your feet. Look at your ankles."

All the kids looked at Mo's ankles and feet. They had turned a bright pink color.

"Does that stuff wash off?" Jessica asked.

Noah turned the hose onto Mo's feet. Nothing happened.

"I guess I need soap," said Mo.

Noah ran into the house and came back out with a bar.

"I bet that didn't happen to Moses and the Israelites," he said. "At least, it doesn't mention it in my book of Bible stories."

It took a lot of soap and a lot of rubbing to get rid of the red coloring. And even so, it looked as if Mo's feet had been sunburned. "I guess it will just have to wear off," Noah said.

"It could have been worse. This could have been the Green Sea," said Jessica.

"There is no Green Sea," said Mo giggling.

"There's a Black Sea," said Andy. "That was the answer to one of the questions on a quiz show last night on TV."

It was just about lunchtime and Mr. Baxter came outside. "I'm going to test this new grill," he told them. "Is there anyone here who'd like an experimental hot dog?"

Everyone cheered. "I'll eat any kind of hot dog. Even an experimental one," said Peter. Actually, he ate two of them.

Later that afternoon, all of Noah's friends had gone off. Noah was lying on his back in a shady corner of the yard reading Mo's copy of *Rip Van Winkle*. Nearby, Bunny was having her turn splashing in the new wading pool.

Suddenly, Noah heard a horrible scream. He jumped up to see what had happened. There was his mother holding Bunny in her arms and yelling.

"She's sick! We've got to get to a doctor at once!" Mrs. Baxter screamed.

Noah's father came running out of the house wrapped in a towel. He'd been taking a shower and his head was covered with shampoo lather.

"What's wrong?" asked Noah. Bunny had been fine just a minute ago.

"I don't know," his mother said. "She doesn't feel hot. But she's turned bright red. We've got to take her to the emergency room at the hospital." She opened the door to the car and strapped Bunny into her seat.

"I just need a second to get some

clothes," Mr. Baxter said, rushing back into the house.

"Wait!" shouted Noah to his father. He had suddenly realized what the problem was. His face turned as red as his sister's skin.

"This is an emergency!" his mother cried out to him. "We can't wait. This is horrible."

"No, it's not. It's food coloring."

"Food coloring? What are you talking about?" his mother shouted out of the open window of the car.

Noah had to explain it a couple of times more before his parents really understood what had happened. "Look," he said pointing to his sister's favorite plush toy that was lying on the ground near the pool. It was a white rabbit that she had named Smashed Potato. Now it had several pink splotches where water had splashed on it.

"Oh no, Noah," Mrs. Baxter scolded her son. "How did you ever think of something so ridiculous?"

Mr. Baxter went for a pair of pants for himself and a bar of soap for Bunny. Mrs. Baxter rubbed it all over her daughter. Luckily, Noah's sister thought it was all a game.

"Bathtime!" she called out over and over again. "Bathtime."

Mrs. Baxter didn't think it was a game at all. "Don't you ever do that again," she told Noah. "You frightened me to death."

"But I didn't," Noah began. Then he stopped himself. He wouldn't squeal on Mo. What would it help? He remembered what Jessica had said earlier. "It could have been worse," he told his mother. "Bunny could have turned green."

When Jessica had said that, all the kids laughed. But his mother didn't think it was funny at all.

"Tato has a boo-boo," said Bunny, calling her toy by its nickname as she stroked the pink spots on her stuffed rabbit.

"Tato needs a visit in the washing machine," said their mother.

Chapter 7
Mo Makes a Move

This summer was the best. With his new friends and his new home, Noah really felt great. Of course, in the back of his mind there was a small worry about starting a new school. But that was still several weeks off, so he tried not to think about it at all.

One morning, Noah was out in the backyard keeping an eye on Bunny. A voice called out to them and then a face popped through the hedge. It was Mo.

"Hi," she shouted. "Guess what?"

Noah shrugged. He wasn't good at guessing.

"I'm moving and getting a new bedroom," Mo announced proudly.

"Moving?" asked Noah dumbfounded. How could Mo move away when they had just become friends?

"Yep. I'm really excited about it. Now I'm going to sleep on the top of the bunk bed. All this time Erin has had the top. But now I will. Isn't that great?"

"When are you moving?" Noah asked.

"Very soon. Before school starts, anyhow."

School! Noah had looked forward to walking to school with Mo. He'd hoped they'd be in the same class. Even if they weren't, they were both going into third grade. They could've done their homework together. His stomach flipped at the thought of going off to his new school without Mo's company.

"Here, Bunny," Mo said, picking up the ball that Noah's sister had been playing with. "Catch."

Bunny couldn't catch the ball but she loved running after it.

Noah sat on the ground and watched. It had never occurred to him that just as he had moved away from his old home, his new friend could move, too. Bunny picked up the ball and threw it toward Noah.

"Come on, lazy. Get the ball," Mo called to him.

Noah got up and went after the ball. He hadn't realized how much he looked forward to seeing Mo's head sticking through his hedge every day. Now she was going away. For an instant he thought that maybe a third-grade boy would move into her house. But suppose it was a family with no kids.

As they continued playing ball, Noah's mind was busy working out all the possibilities. The best one would be if Mo's family changed their minds. Maybe they wouldn't move after all. But he knew that was unlikely. His parents had decided to move and then they moved. That was that.

"Did your parents buy a new house?" he asked Mo.

"Of course not," she replied. "Don't be silly."

"Oh," Noah replied. It hadn't occurred to him that Mo's family was renting their house.

"Will you be very far away?" he asked.

"Just a few feet," Mo said.

Noah didn't understand that at all. He figured they were about six or seven feet apart at that moment. How could Mo move just a few feet away?

He wanted to ask Mo more questions about her new home, but she didn't seem to want to talk about it. Probably she didn't want to move. He remembered he'd felt that way sometimes before his family came here.

"Did you finish my copy of *Rip Van Winkle?*" Mo asked Noah.

"Yeah. I'll get it back to you," Noah said. He should have returned it before this. And now that Mo's family was packing to move, it was no wonder that she was reminding him.

After a while, Mo had to go back through

the hedge to her house. She was going shopping with her mother. "See you later," she called to Noah and Bunny.

"Bye-bye," Bunny called after her.

Noah didn't say anything. He was already thinking of their final good-bye when Mo would move away.

In the afternoon, Peter came by and called for Noah. "We're going to ride our bikes over in the teachers' parking lot by the school. Wanna come?" he asked.

"Okay," Noah said. He told his mother about the plan.

Outside his house were Andy and Jessica, too. "Mo's not home," Peter said.

"She went shopping with her mom," Noah explained. "Did you know she's going to move?" he asked.

"Mo's moving?" asked Jessica. "I didn't know that."

"She just told me this morning," Noah said, as they all started riding single file along the sidewalk toward the parking lot, which was two blocks away.

"How come she told you and she didn't tell me?" Jessica called out. "I thought I was her best friend. I've known her longer than you."

Wow, Noah thought proudly. Mo had told him something that Jessica hadn't known. She must really like him, he thought. Then he realized it didn't matter how much she liked him if she was moving away.

"Maybe she didn't have a chance," Noah told Jessica when they reached the parking lot and they were all standing around supporting their bikes. "Maybe she didn't want to talk about it." He didn't tell Jessica that Mo sounded very happy with her news.

"We'll miss her," Andy said. "She always has good ideas for things to do."

"Yeah. Like the funeral for the deer," said Jessica.

"And making the Red Sea in the wading pool," Peter added.

"I think we should have a good-bye party for her," said Andy. "Because if she moves, she won't be here for her birthday."

"We could do it at our house," offered Jessica. "I know our mom would let us. When is she moving?"

"She didn't know the exact date," said Noah. "Before school opens, she said."

"I know what! Let's make it a surprise party," suggested Jessica. "We could do it next week."

The idea of a surprise party for Mo pleased them all. "We should give her a present to take with her," Noah said.

"Hey," said Andy, "after we finish riding, we could go to my house. My brother's home and he could take a picture of all of us with the camera he got for his birthday. Then we could put the picture in a frame. That would be a perfect good-bye gift."

"Cool," said Peter. "That's a great idea."

So the afternoon was spent bike riding, and Noah practiced riding with no hands. Then they went to Andy's and posed for the farewell picture. In the evening, Jessica phoned Noah and said her mother agreed to a party a week from that day. "Don't forget. It's a surprise. Don't tell Mo," she warned him. "I'm going to invite her to come for lunch. She'll think she's the only one coming over. But I want you and Andy to get here early and hide."

"All right," Noah said. The idea of the party would have been fun if he hadn't been so disappointed that Mo was going away.

"My mother was very surprised about Mo's family moving. She didn't know anything about it and she said she just saw Mo's mom in the post office yesterday," Jessica told Noah.

"Maybe they're sad about leaving and don't want to talk about it," Noah said.

"If they're sad about leaving, then why are they leaving?" Jessica asked.

"I don't know. People have reasons," Noah said. "Sometimes they're private."

He remembered again how he'd felt both happy and scared at the same time before his family had moved here.

On the morning of the surprise party it looked like rain. Mo came over to Noah's house to hang out, but he had a hard time getting rid of her. "Don't you have any plans for today?" he asked her. He needed to get over to their friends' house before Mo did.

"Yeah. I'm going to have lunch with Jessica and Peter," she said. "They said to come at noon."

Noah was supposed to be there at eleven-thirty and it was already eleven o'clock.

"Maybe your mother needs you to help her," he said.

"Naw. She told me to go outside because it's time for Kitty's nap and I was making too much noise."

"Well, I think I may have to walk over to the supermarket and get something for my mother," Noah said.

"Okay. I'll go with you."

"But we might not get back in time. You'll be late for Jessica."

"Are you crazy? It only takes ten minutes

to get to the supermarket. Even if there is a long line, it wouldn't take more than twenty minutes to buy whatever you want and get back here. I'd still be early for lunch at Jessica's."

"Oh." Noah watched the clock. It was ten after eleven. Then it was eleven-fifteen. He only needed about two minutes to get over to Jessica's, but he needed Mo to disappear so he could do it.

"I'll be right back," Noah said. He went looking for his mother. She, too, had been surprised that their neighbors were moving so suddenly. "If I'd known they were leaving, I would have told Aunt Julia and Uncle Edward to come and look at it."

Now Noah told her about his problem. It turned out he had two problems, not one.

"Oh no, Noah, I forgot to tell you," his

mother said. "Mo isn't moving away. You must have misunderstood her. I asked her mother about it, and she said they had no plans for leaving the neighborhood."

"She's not moving?" Noah asked, stunned. "But she has to move. She told me she was. We're planning a good-bye party. It's a surprise. That's why I have to get over to Jessica and Peter's house."

"I thought you'd be pleased that Mo is staying around," Mrs. Baxter said.

"Well, I am. But I don't know how I'll explain it to the other kids."

"You'll think of something," his mother reassured him. They whispered together for a moment, and then Noah went back to Mo.

The clock read twenty-two minutes after eleven.

"Oooo! Ouch!" Noah called out suddenly.

"What's the matter?" asked Mo.

"I've got a toothache," said Noah, holding on to his right cheek. He'd seen someone do that in a movie once.

"Mom, Mom," he shouted. "Can you take me to the dentist right away? I have a terrible toothache."

"Just a minute," Mrs. Baxter called. She picked up Bunny in one arm and grabbed her pocketbook with the other. "Sorry Mo, we're going to have to run off," she said to Noah's friend.

"Poor Noah," Mo said. "What dentist do you use?"

"Dr. Millman," said Noah, remembering the name of their dentist when they lived in the city.

"Dr. Shapiro," said Mrs. Baxter, giving the name of a local dentist who had been recommended to her by Mo's mother.

"Which one?" Mo asked, puzzled.

"Dr. Shapiro," said Noah.

"Dr. Millman," said Mrs. Baxter.

"Oooo. Ouch. Take me to either one. Fast," Noah begged.

Mrs. Baxter held the door open. Mo walked out first, followed by Mrs. Baxter holding Bunny. Noah was last, holding on to his cheek.

So at eleven thirty-five, Noah was at neither Dr. Millman's nor Dr. Shapiro's office but at Jessica and Peter's house.

At noon, when Mo arrived, Andy and Noah jumped out from behind the sofa in the living room. "Surprise!" they shouted.

Only Noah knew that it was everyone else who was going to be surprised in a couple of minutes. He still hadn't admitted his silly mistake to the others.

Mo looked puzzled. "Why aren't you at

the dentist?" she asked, looking at Noah. "And why are you surprising me? It's not my birthday or anything."

"It's a good-bye party," Jessica explained.

"Good-bye? Good-bye to what?"

"Good-bye to you. We're sorry that you're moving away. And we want to be sure you'll always remember us," said Jessica. She handed Mo a flat package wrapped in a floral gift wrap.

"I'm not moving anywhere," said Mo. But that didn't stop her from ripping open the paper. Inside was a wooden frame with a picture of Peter, Andy, Jessica, and Noah grinning together.

"This is a neat picture," said Mo. "I wish I was in it."

"What do you mean you're not moving?" asked Peter.

"This is a surprise good-bye lunch for you," said Jessica.

"Well, I'm sort of moving. But I'm not moving very far. I'm not moving out of my house," Mo explained.

"Well, where are you moving?" Jessica wanted to know.

"I'm moving to another bedroom inside my house. Erin begged and begged my parents to have her own bedroom. So we're switching all the rooms around. She's going to sleep in the little room where Kitty sleeps now. And Kitty and I are going into the big bedroom where my parents sleep, and my parents are moving into the bedroom where Erin and I sleep. And I'm going to sleep on top of the bunk bed, which I've been wanting to do forever and ever. So we're all moving around. But we're not moving very far."

"Wait a minute," said Andy. "I'm all confused. You mean you're not moving away from this neighborhood?" he asked.

"Nope."

"And you'll still be going to the same school?" asked Peter.

"Yep."

Jessica looked at Noah. "Oh no, Noah. You got it all wrong," she said.

"I know," Noah finally admitted. "My mother told me just before I came here. But it was too late to call off the party," he said. "Besides, aren't you glad that I made a mistake?"

"I'm glad you don't really have a toothache," Mo told him.

"I have a question," said Andy.

"Yeah?" they all asked him.

"Can we still have lunch even if Mo isn't moving?"

"Sure," said Jessica beaming. "It'll be a *we're happy no one's moving away party*."

"And we're happy Noah moved here, too," Mo reminded all of them.

Noah was happy, too.

Chapter 8
Another Party

By the end of August, the Baxter family felt very much at home in their new house. All the furniture was in place, the boxes unpacked, books shelved, and the curtains and pictures hung. The house no longer smelled of fresh paint. Instead, faint cooking aromas scented the air. The house looked and smelled like home. It was time to celebrate.

Noah's parents sent out invitations to family and friends. They were going to have a party. Mr. Baxter was proud of the barbecue grill he'd bought and each evening he practiced cooking something new on it—hot dogs, hamburgers, steak, chops, fish, and even roasted fresh vegetables. Now he planned a menu to cook when the guests came.

"You're like a kid with a new toy," Mrs. Baxter told him.

"I just hope it doesn't rain," her husband said as they planned for the party. They had invited about thirty people. There would be room for them in the house, but it would be much better if people could move freely indoors and out.

The morning of the housewarming party arrived with bright sunshine. It was warm, but not beastly hot. The cans of soda were keeping cold in the washing machine, which had been filled with ice cubes. Mrs. Baxter had bought bread, cookies, and six large fruit pies at the local bakery. From a nearby farm stand, she had bought fresh tomatoes, cucumbers, and corn. It was going to be a wonderful party.

Noah was excited because two of his old best friends, Kenny and Jon, were coming with their parents. He'd spoken with the brothers on the telephone, but he hadn't seen them all summer. Mo and her parents were coming, too. They would bring Kitty, but Mo's big sister had a play date with one of her friends.

By three o'clock, there were four cars squeezed into their driveway and a whole line of other vehicles all up and down

Rainbow Drive. It was very satisfying to look at all those cars and to know that they all belonged to friends.

Just when the hamburgers began sizzling on the grill, Mo poked her nose through the hedge.

"Hi," she called to Noah. "My parents are walking around the block to come in your front door. But here I am."

Noah grabbed his new friend by the arm to take her to meet his old friends who had just arrived. Within minutes all four of them were playing tag out in front of the house. But when the smell of the hamburgers and hot dogs wafted from the backyard to the front, they called a halt. Time to fuel up.

They took their plates filled with food and cans of soda and sat on the front steps, away from all the grown-ups. They didn't talk much because they were so busy eating. But Noah looked up and noticed a black Camry driving very slowly down their street and then turning at the corner and driving back again.

Mo saw it, too. "Do you think that's another guest?" she asked. "You sure know a lot of people."

"This is nothing," said Noah. "When my grandparents celebrated their fortieth wedding anniversary, there was a humongous party with almost a hundred people."

As he spoke, he watched as the Camry finally stopped at the far end of the street. He didn't recognize the car or the tall man who got out with a woman and a little girl.

"So, do you know them?" Kenny asked.

Noah shook his head. "Nope," he said,

chewing a mouthful of hamburger. "They must be visiting someone else. We're not the only family on this street, you know."

Still, he watched as the three strangers walked closer and closer to his house.

Then the man, woman, and little girl stopped right in front of them.

"Number 412," the man said, reading the numbers nailed onto the door. "This is it. 412 Rainbow Drive. And I bet one of you fellows must be Noah Baxter."

Kenny, Jon, and Mo all pointed to Noah. Noah didn't say anything.

"Hi," the man said. "I'm George Powers. I work with your dad."

Noah froze. George Powers was the man who had given them the deer head.

"Does my dad know you're coming?" Noah asked, which, even as he said it, he

knew was not a very friendly way to greet visitors to one's home.

"He invited us," Mr. Powers said, smiling at Noah. "But we didn't think we could make it. We were supposed to go somewhere else today, but that plan fell through. And so, here we are."

"Hi Noah," the woman said, smiling. "This is Hilary. I think you have a little sister who's close to her in age."

Noah nodded his head. Then, finally, remembering his manners, he stood up. "My parents and most of the guests are in the backyard," he said. "I'll show you." Maybe if the Powers stayed in the backyard eating and talking with other people, they wouldn't go inside looking for the deer head. Noah hadn't thought much about that old head in recent weeks. His parents seemed to have forgotten about it, too. But he was very much afraid that Mr. Powers wouldn't have forgotten about it at all. In fact, he probably came today especially to have a look at it. And one thing Noah knew for certain: Mr. Powers could look all he wanted, but he wasn't going to find it.

Chapter 9
Another Gift

"George, what a surprise!" Mr. Baxter said when he saw George Powers. Putting down the grilling utensil in his right hand, he wiped his hand on his apron and then extended it toward his guest. His face was already flushed from standing over the grill, but Noah saw it get redder still.

"I know I said we couldn't make it, but we had a change in plans. And I'm eager to see your new home," said Mr. Powers.

Noah couldn't bear to hear what the men would say next. He raced back to the front of the house, where his friends were finishing the food on their plates.

"That's the man," Noah said to Mo.

"What man?" asked Mo puzzled.

"The one who gave us the head," Noah explained.

"What head?" asked Kenny.

"The one we buried," said Noah. "We had a funeral."

"It was great," said Mo. "Just like a real one."

"What head?" Kenny asked again. "A real head?"

"You buried a head?" Jon said. "How could you bury a head? Wasn't there a body?"

"Just a head, no body," said Noah. "But what am I going to do now?"

"What head?" asked Kenny still another time.

"A stuffed deer head. It was a gift from Mr. Powers. And now he's going to want to see it hanging up on our wall. And it won't be there."

Mo filled in the blanks for Kenny and Jon. She told them about the gift that had been hidden in the basement.

"Wait a minute," said Jon. "Even if you didn't have a funeral, if it was hidden in the basement, it wouldn't be up on the wall for Mr. Powers to see."

"That's right," said Mo, grinning. "So you're in the clear. You don't have to worry. Your dad will probably tell him that he didn't have a chance to hang it up yet. It takes a long time to get everything fixed up after you move to a new house."

"Sure," said Kenny. "I don't think you have to worry about anything." He paused. "Are they serving dessert yet?" he asked.

"Let's go look," said Mo.

Noah looked at Mo. How could she think about dessert when she'd gotten him in such hot water? It had been her idea to hold the funeral for the deer head, not his.

The four kids took their paper plates to throw into the trash and walked around to the back of the house. Three of them went looking for dessert. But Noah was looking for Mr. Powers. He saw Mr. Powers's little daughter playing with Bunny and Kitty. The three girls were chasing one another around a tree. Noah saw Mrs. Powers sitting on a lawn chair with a plate of food, talking to some of the other women. Where was Mr. Powers?

Noah had a feeling he was inside the house. He also had the feeling that no matter what his friends said, he was about to get into big trouble. In fact, he already was in big trouble and he didn't know how he'd get out of it.

The back door opened and Mr. Powers came out. "Well, you certainly found yourself a lovely home," he said to Noah's mom. "But I noticed you haven't found a spot to hang the deer head yet. I think it would look perfect over your fireplace."

"Yes, you're probably right," said Mrs. Baxter, smiling politely. "We've put it away temporarily, but by the next time you come for a visit, it will be up."

"Sure," said Noah's dad. "It will be the first thing anyone sees when they enter our living room."

"Did I overhear that you have a deer head?" asked Kenny and Jon's dad. "My grandfather had one hanging in his house when I was a kid. I remember that I was fascinated by it."

"Yes," said Noah's father. "It is something that could fascinate you."

"I'd really love to see it sometime," Jon's father commented. "I haven't seen one recently."

"Well," began Mrs. Baxter. "It's in the basement, but we could take you down there to see it."

"Oh, bring it upstairs," suggested Mr. Powers. "I bet a lot of your guests would find it interesting."

"Oh really, George. What are you thinking of?" said Mrs. Powers, standing up and walking over to her husband. "If it's down in the basement, leave it there. We don't need to see that old thing in the middle of a festive occasion like this."

"It's no trouble at all," said Mr. Baxter. He called to his son. "Noah, you remember where I put the carton with the deer's head? Would you bring it outside, please."

Noah walked over to his father. "It scares Bunny," he whispered to him. Maybe, just maybe, he could avoid bringing the box up from the basement.

Mrs. Powers overheard the whisper. "See George, what did I tell you?" she asked her husband.

If they managed to avoid showing the deer head now, what would happen next time Mr. Powers came to visit? Noah wondered. What would they tell him next time?

"Don't worry about Bunny," said Mr. Baxter. "She's busy playing with Hilary and Kitty. Please bring up the box, Noah."

Noah stood frozen for a moment. What could he do? He looked over and saw Mo busy eating dessert. She'd gotten him into this mess. But he could see she wasn't going to help him get out. He glared at her.

There seemed nothing for him to do but go downstairs to the basement. After the funeral, he'd put the empty carton back where it had been. Now he went over to it and opened the box. It would have been an incredible miracle if the deer head was back inside. But of course, there was no miracle. The box was empty.

Noah took off his glasses and rubbed his eyes. He could hide the box under a pile of others that were there and say he couldn't find it. He could say it was missing. He could say someone had stolen it. He sighed and put his glasses back on. Whatever he said would only postpone telling what he'd done. Noah sat down on the basement floor.

After a couple of minutes he heard someone calling his name. "Noah? Are you down here?" It was Mo.

"Yeah," Noah said. He looked up and saw Mo coming down the stairs with Kenny and Jon.

The three friends sat down on the floor next to Noah. They sat there for a few minutes in the dimly lit basement until Jon spoke up. "Why are we sitting here?"

"This is where the deer head was. Before it was buried at the funeral. When I go upstairs and tell my parents what I did, I'm going to get in really big, big trouble."

"Yeah," said Mo.

"But you can't just sit down here in the basement all afternoon," said Jon.

"Or for the rest of your life," said Kenny.

"Better go upstairs and get it over with," said Mo. "Come on," she said, jumping up.

Reluctantly, Noah got up off the floor. He picked up the empty carton because it felt better to have something in his hands. Then he led the others up the basement steps.

"Here's Noah," Mr. Baxter called out cheerfully. "You were gone so long that I began to think you might have gotten lost down in the basement."

Noah wished he had gotten lost down there. He put the box down on the ground. His father bent down to open it up.

"No, wait!" Noah shouted.

"What's the problem?" his father asked.

"The head isn't inside. It's gone."

"Gone? Where could it go?"

"It's my fault," Noah admitted. "I took it."

"Oh no, Noah. What did you do?" his mother asked him.

"It had a funeral and it's buried," said Noah softly.

"What?" gasped his mother.

"He didn't do anything. I did. I took it," said Mo, stepping forward and taking hold of Noah's hand.

"You took it? Where did you take it? Where is it buried?" asked Mrs. Baxter, puzzled.

"Well, it was dead, wasn't it?" Mo asked.

"Of course it was dead," said Mr. Baxter. "What's that got to do with anything?"

"Everything," said Mo. "We had a funeral. And it was all my idea. I've always wanted to have a funeral."

"A funeral? How could there be a funeral?" asked both of Noah's parents together. As for Mr. Powers, he didn't say anything at all. He stood with his hands on his hips, looking at the kids.

"It was easy," Noah explained. He was amazed that Mo had come forward to share the blame. He could hardly believe that she was standing next to him holding his hand. But after all, the funeral had been a group effort. "I thought it was a good plan," said Noah. "After all, the head was dead."

"It was dead," said Mrs. Powers, breaking her silence. "It was certainly dead."

"Did you kill it?" Noah asked Mr. Powers.

"No, not me. I'm not a hunter," said Mr. Powers.

"Then where did it come from?" asked Mo.

"To tell you the truth, I bought it at a

garage sale. I saw it the very weekend you people moved in here and I thought it would be an original gift."

"It wasn't original, it was ridiculous," said Mrs. Powers. "George brought that head home and I told him that he couldn't hang it in any house I lived in. And when Hilary saw it," she added, pointing to her daughter who was still playing with Bunny, "she screamed so loud, he put it back in the box. Afterward he said he'd give it to you. He said he thought you'd appreciate it better than I did. But I see he was wrong about that." She turned to her husband. "I think a funeral was the proper fate for that poor old deer."

Noah and Mo described the funeral. They mentioned the prayer and they mentioned the songs. But they didn't tell where the head was buried. Noah didn't think it would be right to dig the head up. He also didn't say he was sorry. He wasn't sorry at all.

"I hope you didn't pay a lot of money for that head," said Mrs. Baxter, looking at her husband's supervisor with embarrassment, after she had heard the full story from Noah and Mo.

"Actually, I paid very little," said Mr. Powers. "In fact, I think the people having the garage sale would have paid me to take it from them. Deer heads don't seem to be so popular these days," he admitted.

"Does that mean you aren't angry with us?" asked Noah hopefully.

Mr. Powers looked at Noah and began laughing. "Don't worry," he said. "I'm not angry. I'm just sorry that I wasn't invited to the funeral."

"Maybe we could dig up the head and do

it again," he offered after all. But he was relieved when all the adults said, "No, no, no," in unison.

"Actually, we have something else for your family," said Mr. Powers.

"Oh dear, now you have a reason to worry," called out Mrs. Powers. But she was laughing. "We have it with us. It's in the car, but I insisted that we check it out with your parents before we delivered it."

"What is it?" asked Noah nervously. Maybe this was something else they'd have to hide in the basement or bury in Andy's backyard.

Mr. and Mrs. Powers pulled Mr. and Mrs. Baxter aside to speak to them. The adults whispered together for a minute.

"What do you think the new present is?" Mo asked Noah. She had walked over carrying a plate with her second piece of peach pie on it and she had overheard the last few words that the Powers had said.

Noah shrugged his shoulders. He didn't have too much faith in Mr. Powers's idea of a good gift. "More wineglasses?" he guessed. "Or a dead cow."

When his parents and the Powerses finished their conversation, Mr. Powers went off to their car. While he was gone, Mr. Baxter pulled his son off to one side. "Listen, Noah," he said. "I hope you don't have any other plans in mind that you haven't discussed with us. You weren't planning to bury your mother's jewelry as pirate treasure, for example, were you?"

"Oh, could I?" asked Noah eagerly.

"Oh no, Noah. I was only joking," said Mr. Baxter. "Don't you dare bury it."

"I was only joking, too," said Noah, grinning at his father.

Just then, Mr. Powers came back carrying a carton. From the outside it looked just like the box that had once held the deer head. But the top was open and there was a scratching sound from within.

Mr. Powers put the carton down on the ground. Noah and his friends all stooped to look inside.

It was not a deer head. It was a very small kitten. And it was very much alive. The kitten was striped like a tiger and soft as a bunny.

"This is a fantastic present," said Noah with delight. "Can we really, really keep it?" he asked his parents.

"I don't see why not," said his father.

Noah gently lifted the kitten from the

box. It was so small that it fit right into the palm of his hand. "Thanks a lot," he told the Powerses.

Bunny came running over to look at their new pet. "Kitty!" she shrieked with delight.

"What will we call it? Is it a boy or a girl?" Noah asked.

"Female," said Mrs. Powers. "Our cat just gave birth to a litter of four kittens. Three female and one male. She's six weeks old and ready to leave her mother."

"Kitty," shouted Bunny again. "Her name's Kitty."

It wasn't a very clever or original name. But it was a darling kitten. Everyone agreed.

"Lucky stiff," said Mo, petting the kitten and looking at Noah.

Noah nodded his head. He knew he was. "You can play with her whenever you come over," he promised.

"I will," said Mo.

"But I think you should start thinking about a pet of your own. If my sister is called Bunny and she has a Kitty, don't you think your sister Kitty should have a . . ."

"Bunny!" called out Mo.

"Bingo," said Noah.

"No, no," said Kenny, stroking the kitten. "Bingo is the name of a dog."

Noah put the new kitten back in the safety of the box. Now he was ready to have some dessert, too, if there was any left. Even if he didn't get any, he wouldn't be upset. Everything had worked out fine. Better than fine, he thought. It was great the way Mo had admitted to her part in the funeral and shared the blame with him. It showed they were real friends. In fact, his parents may have received a load of house-warming presents since they moved to their new home, but Noah knew for certain that he had gotten the best gift of all—a set of new friends, especially Mo.

There was a slight breeze and he noticed a single leaf floating slowly down from one of the trees in the yard. Soon autumn would be here and school would be opening. The thought of starting a new school was still a little scary. But having gotten out of hot water this afternoon, Noah didn't think anything nearly as terrible was in his future. In fact, going to school with Mo and the others would be lots of fun.

Noah got to the dessert table just in time to get the last slice of peach pie. Oh yes.